For Aunty Vicky and Uncle Roger

A Red Fox Book
Published by Random House Children's Books
20 Vauxhall Bridge Road, London SW1V 2SA
A division of Random House UK Ltd
London Melbourne Sydney Auckland
Johannesburg and agencies throughout the world
Copyright © Gus Clarke 1995
1 3 5 7 9 10 6 4 2
First Published in Great Britain by Andersen Press Ltd 1995
Red Fox edition 1999
Printed in Hong Kong
Random House UK Limited Reg. No. 954009
ISBN 0 09 926255 X

TOO MANY TEDDIES

Gus Clarke

RED FOX

"Mum," said Frank. "There are just too many teddies."

"Nonsense," said Mum. "You can never have too many teddies."

But Frank did.

It started the day he was born. "A boy needs a bear," said Uncle Jim. And that was the first . . .

... of many.

He'd get them for birthdays and for Christmas ...

... for all sorts of special occasions ...

and sometimes for no particular reason at all.

By the time he was four there was more than a bed full. There were teddies everywhere.

And even the teddies had teddies.

At bedtime his dad would tuck them all in and together they would say goodnight to them. One by one.

It seemed to Frank that if he got many more teddies, by the time they'd said goodnight to them all it would be time to get up!

It was then that Frank knew he'd really got a problem. But the more he thought about it, the more he could see that the problem was not the teddies ...

... the problem was Dad ... and Mum ...

and all the aunties and uncles, the grandmas and grandpas, the cousins, the friends and the neighbours that kept on giving him all these teddies.

He knew that they all liked teddies and he knew that they all liked choosing the teddies. They'd told him.

They'd spend ages choosing the cuddliest one, or the cutest one, the furriest or the funniest one, the one with the special smile ...

... or even just the one with the squeakiest tummy.

In fact, just the sort of teddy that they would like for themselves. But, of course, being so grown up they thought they couldn't really buy it for themselves.

So they bought it for Frank. At least they could have a little cuddle before they gave it to him.

And that was when he had his idea. Perhaps, thought Frank, if they all had a teddy of their own to cuddle, they wouldn't need to buy quite so many for him.

"Grandma," said Frank. "Would you like to look after my teddy for a little while? I've got plenty more."

And, of course, Grandma was only too pleased.

And so was Aunty Vicky ... and Uncle Roger ...

... and Cousin Percy ...

and the man next door but one. And everyone else.

Of course, Frank kept one or two for himself – his favourites, and one or two more to keep them company.

And that was that. They all lived happily ever after. Until one day ...

"A boy needs a dog," said Uncle Jim.

And that . . .

... was the first of many.

Some bestselling Red Fox picture books

THE BIG ALFIE AND ANNIE ROSE STORYBOOK
by Shirley Hughes
OLD BEAR
by Jane Hissey
OI! GET OFF OUR TRAIN
by John Burningham
DON'T DO THAT!
by Tony Ross
NOT NOW, BERNARD
by David McKee
ALL JOIN IN
by Quentin Blake
THE WHALES' SONG
by Gary Blythe and Dyan Sheldon
JESUS' CHRISTMAS PARTY
by Nicholas Allan
THE PATCHWORK CAT
by Nicola Bayley and William Mayne
WILLY AND HUGH
by Anthony Browne
THE WINTER HEDGEHOG
by Ann and Reg Cartwright
A DARK, DARK TALE
by Ruth Brown
HARRY, THE DIRTY DOG
by Gene Zion and Margaret Bloy Graham
DR XARGLE'S BOOK OF EARTHLETS
by Jeanne Willis and Tony Ross
WHERE'S THE BABY?
by Pat Hutchins